EDGE BOOKS

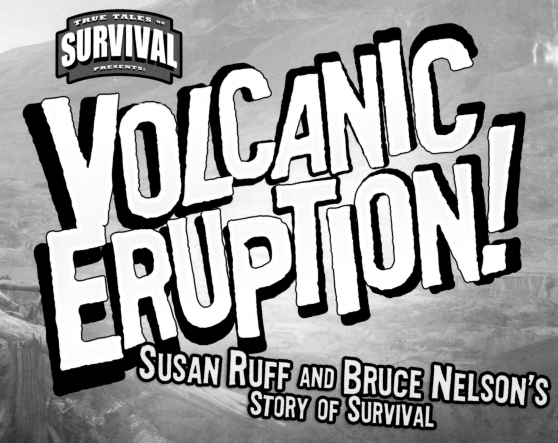

TRUE TALES OF SURVIVAL PRESENTS:

VOLCANIC ERUPTION!

SUSAN RUFF AND BRUCE NELSON'S STORY OF SURVIVAL

by Tim O'Shei

Consultant:
Al Siebert, PhD
Author of *The Survivor Personality*

Capstone press
Mankato, Minnesota

Edge Books are published by Capstone Press,
151 Good Counsel Drive, P.O. Box 669, Mankato, Minnesota 56002.
www.capstonepress.com

Library of Congress Cataloging-in-Publication Data
O'Shei, Tim.
  Volcanic eruption!: Susan Ruff and Bruce Nelson's story of survival / by
Tim O'Shei.
  p. cm.—(Edge books. True tales of survival)
  Summary: "Describes how campers Sue Ruff and Bruce Nelson survived the
1980 eruption of Mount St. Helens"—Provided by publisher.
  Includes bibliographical references and index.
  ISBN-13: 978-0-7368-6779-5 (hardcover)
  ISBN-10: 0-7368-6779-1 (hardcover)
  ISBN-13: 978-0-7368-7869-2 (softcover pbk.)
  ISBN-10: 0-7368-7869-6 (softcover pbk.)
  1. Saint Helens, Mount (Wash.)—Eruption, 1980—Juvenile literature.
2. Volcanic eruptions—Saint Helens, Mount—Juvenile literature. 3. Wilderness
survival—Saint Helens, Mount—Juvenile literature. I. Title. II. Series.
QE523.S23O55 2007
979.7'84—dc22   2006024769

Editorial Credits
Angie Kaelberer, editor; Jason Knudson, designer; Wanda Winch, photo
    researcher/photo editor

Photo Credits
AP/Wide World Photos, 10, 18–19; Courtesy USDA Forest Service, Mount St. Helens
    National Volcanic Monument, 28; Mike Cash, 14–15
Corbis/Bettmann, 20–21, 24–25; David Muench, 4; Douglas Kirkland, 16;
    Gary Braasch, 26–27; Jim Sugar, 22–23; Steve Terrill, 6–7
Photodisc, cover
Shutterstock, 12–13 (background), 28–29 (background); coko, 2–3; Gina Goforth,
    8–9 (background); Guy Erwood, 16–17 (background), 32; Robert O. Brown
    Photography, back cover; Ronald Sherwood, 1; Valeriy Poltorak, 30–31
The Daily News/Roger Werth, 8, 12 (both)
USGS/Austin Post, 11; Cascades Volcano Observatory/Lyn Topinka, 29

1 2 3 4 5 6 12 11 10 09 08 07

TABLE OF CONTENTS

CHAPTER 1

NIGHTMARE IN THE WOODS

LEARN ABOUT:
- A PEACEFUL MORNING
- THE WORLD EXPLODES
- A BLACK CLOUD

4

Before May 1980, Mount St. Helens overlooked peaceful Spirit Lake.

"Bruce! There's a fire!"

When he woke up on Sunday, May 18, 1980, Bruce Nelson thought he was going to have a good day. He was camping with five friends along the Green River in Washington. Large fir trees towered over their tents.

It was 8:30 in the morning. Bruce and his girlfriend, Sue Ruff, were eating toasted marshmallows for breakfast. Their friend Terry Crall was fishing in the Green River. Campers Brian Thomas, Karen Varner, and Danny Balch were still in their tents.

Just two minutes later, a cold wind rushed through the campsite. The campfire flames shot sideways.

"Bruce!" Terry yelled. "There's a fire!"

6

A towering cloud of ash filled the
sky as the mountain burst open.

Bruce and Sue looked to the sky. A massive cloud of white smoke loomed above them. But it wasn't a firecloud. Suddenly, the cloud turned yellow, red, and black. The cloud spread outward, as if it had arms. Everything turned dark. Bruce grabbed Sue, wrapping his arms around her.

So much for peace. After the eruption, their day—and their lives—were about to change.

EDGE FACT

The eruption of Mount St. Helens was so strong that people felt it 200 miles (320 kilometers) away.

CHAPTER 2

FIRE IN THE SKY

LEARN ABOUT:
- OUTSIDE THE RED ZONE
- EARTHQUAKE!
- NOWHERE TO RUN

The area within 10 miles (16 kilometers) of the volcano was called the Red Zone.

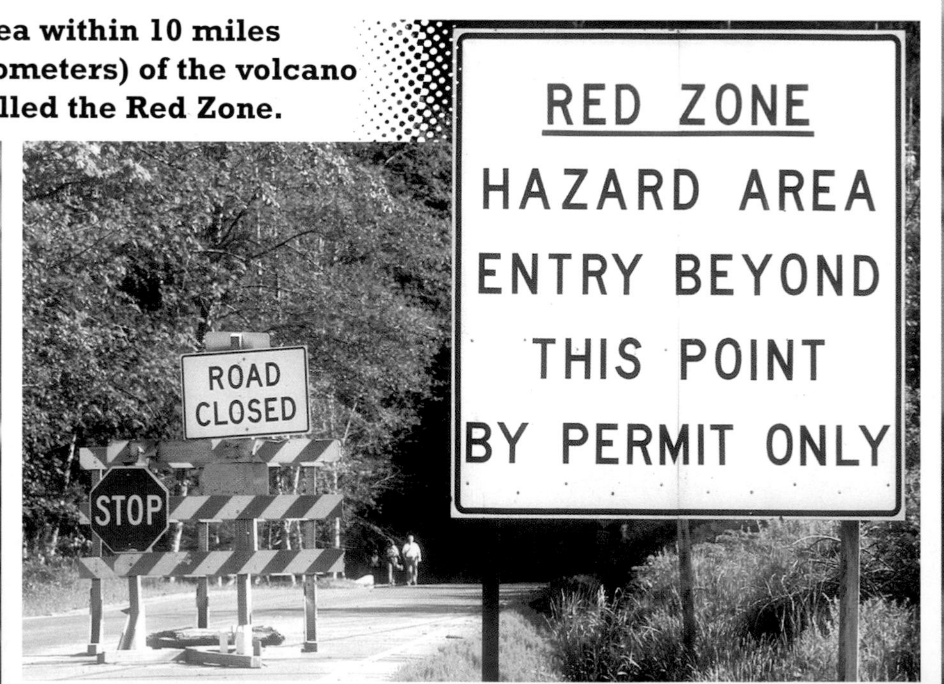

RED ZONE
HAZARD AREA
ENTRY BEYOND
THIS POINT
BY PERMIT ONLY

ROAD CLOSED

STOP

The campers didn't all know each other before the trip. Bruce and Sue had been dating about six months. Karen, Terry, and Brian were friends of Sue's. Brian convinced his friend Danny to come along, too. Terry also brought his dog and her three puppies.

In the short time they spent together, the six campers became close friends. They loved the campsite. A green carpet of moss lined the riverbank. Some of the cedar trees were so huge that two people could join hands and still not circle the trunk.

Mount St. Helens stood 14 miles (23 kilometers) from the campsite, hidden by the ridge of another mountain. The volcano had been rumbling and steaming for about two months, but the campers weren't worried. St. Helens hadn't had a major eruption since 1857. Government officials warned people to stay at least 10 miles (16 kilometers) away from the volcano in case it did erupt. The campers were well outside that zone.

The earthquake that triggered the explosion measured 5.1 on the Richter scale.

TICKING TIME BOMB

As the campers started their day, Mount St. Helens was quietly boiling. For weeks, small earthquakes had loosened the rock and ice that capped the volcanic mountain. Inside were gases and melted rock, or magma. The hot magma was under a great deal of pressure. A big earthquake would shake the cap off the volcano, releasing the magma and gases inside.

That earthquake hit at 8:32 on the morning of May 18. Searing gas with a temperature of 660 degrees Fahrenheit (350 degrees Celsius) burst outward. Burning ash shot nearly 12 miles (19 kilometers) into the sky. Melted snow caused massive mudslides. Chunks of rock and ice soared through the air like missiles.

The volcano spewed hot ash and smoke into two layers of Earth's atmosphere.

The explosion toppled trees and split the **Coal Banks Bridge** in half.

The ash and mud from the volcano left a logging camp in ruins.

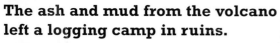

EVERYTHING GOES BLACK

As Bruce watched the ash cloud speed toward him and Sue, it hit a mountain bluff and split into two. Terry ran to Karen's tent. Danny woke up and yelled to Brian, "Let's get out of here!"

The force of the explosion snapped tall trees like toothpicks. Chunks of ice, some the size of cars, crashed to the ground. Rocks both big and small rained from the sky. The noise level was incredible. Sue later said it was like 100 trains all chugging at once.

Bruce and Sue fell into a hole where two uprooted trees had been. It was pitch black. They could hear each other but couldn't see anything. As fallen trees stacked up over the hole, Bruce had only one thought: we're going to die.

EDGE FACT

The explosion heated the Green River to 100 degrees Fahrenheit (38 degrees Celsius). Fish tried to jump out of the water to escape the heat.

CHAPTER 3

STRUGGLING TO SAFETY

LEARN ABOUT:
- **SURVIVING THE BLAST**
- **LUCKY RESCUE**
- **A SAD DISCOVERY**

The ash darkened skies hundreds of miles away from the volcano.

The explosion scorched the countryside. Bruce, who worked as a baker, knew high temperatures well. He estimated that the heat rose as high as 300 degrees Fahrenheit (149 degrees Celsius).

Hot ash fell from the sky. The fallen trees covering the hole protected Bruce and Sue. The hair on their heads and arms was singed, but they didn't suffer serious burns.

As they dug out of the hole, Bruce told Sue that he thought they were going to die. "Nonsense!" she replied.

As Bruce and Sue crawled from the hole, their mouths were full of dirt. Stones fell from the sky, pelting their heads and bodies. They gagged from the smell of the poisonous gases in the air. The ash was so thick that they couldn't see their hands. They tied their sweatshirts around their mouths to keep from breathing in the gases and ash.

Thick ash covered the ground and choked the rivers.

SEARCHING FOR SURVIVORS

When the steady fall of ash started to lighten, Bruce and Sue started looking for their friends. They heard a noise and followed it up a hill. There, they found Danny and Brian. Severe burns covered Danny's arms. A tree limb had crushed Brian's hip. Terry and Karen, last seen in their tent, were nowhere to be found.

The four friends decided to look for help. Brian was too hurt to move much, so the others put him in an old mine shack. They promised to return for him.

Bruce, Sue, and Danny began hiking, hoping to find rescuers. Danny was barefoot and couldn't step on the hot ash. Instead, he hobbled along on fallen tree trunks. Sometimes he stepped into the river to cool his burns. Soon, Danny realized he could go no farther without shoes. Bruce and Sue went ahead, promising to come back for him.

HIKING THROUGH HOT ASH

Bruce and Sue trudged along for hours. In places, the ash was up to their knees. The ash polluted the river and puddles, leaving them no clean water to drink. They still heard explosions and worried that the volcano would erupt again. But they kept moving.

Rescue workers found Sue (second from left), Bruce (middle), and Grant (far right).

18

Bruce and Sue came across a 60-year-old logger named Grant Christensen. The three hiked together, looking for signs of rescuers. About 12 hours after the eruption, they saw a helicopter overhead. Beating their sweatshirts into the ash, they created a smoke plume that wafted into the sky. The pilot saw the signal and landed.

Bruce, Sue, and Grant were about 20 miles (32 kilometers) from the campsite. Sue and Bruce learned that Danny had sent the pilot to find them. After they split up, Danny met a camper named Buzz Smith and his two young sons.

EDGE FACT

In 1980, Bruce Nelson was 22. Sue Ruff was 21. Their friends were also in their early 20s.

Bruce and Sue refused to get into the helicopter unless the pilot promised to also help Brian.

Soldiers searching the area in a helicopter rescued the group, and Danny told the pilot about Sue and Bruce.

But Bruce knew Brian was still deep in the forest. Bruce and Sue refused to get into the helicopter unless the pilot promised to also help Brian. They argued with the pilot until he agreed to broadcast a message on his radio about Brian. Another helicopter pilot heard the message and rescued Brian.

21

Army helicopters searched the disaster area for survivors.

EDGE FACT

The blast blew away
1,313 feet (400 meters) of the
mountaintop. That's longer
than four football fields! Today,
the mountain is 8,364 feet
(2,549 meters) tall.

Downed trees and ash were all that
was left of a mighty forest.

ONE MORE SEARCH

No traces of Karen and Terry were found the day of the rescue. Government officials wouldn't let Bruce go back to the campsite to look for them. But Bruce came up with another plan. Three days after the eruption, Bruce did an interview for *The Today Show*. He talked the TV crew into flying him back to the site. Bruce's one condition was that the crew couldn't film footage of Terry and Karen.

At the campsite two days later, Bruce made a sad discovery. He found Terry and Karen's tent. Both of them were inside, dead. They were huddled in each other's arms. They appeared to be trying to protect each other from the falling trees that killed them.

But Bruce did make a rescue at the campsite. He found Terry's dog and her three puppies, which were unharmed. Saving the dogs gave him a small reason to be happy.

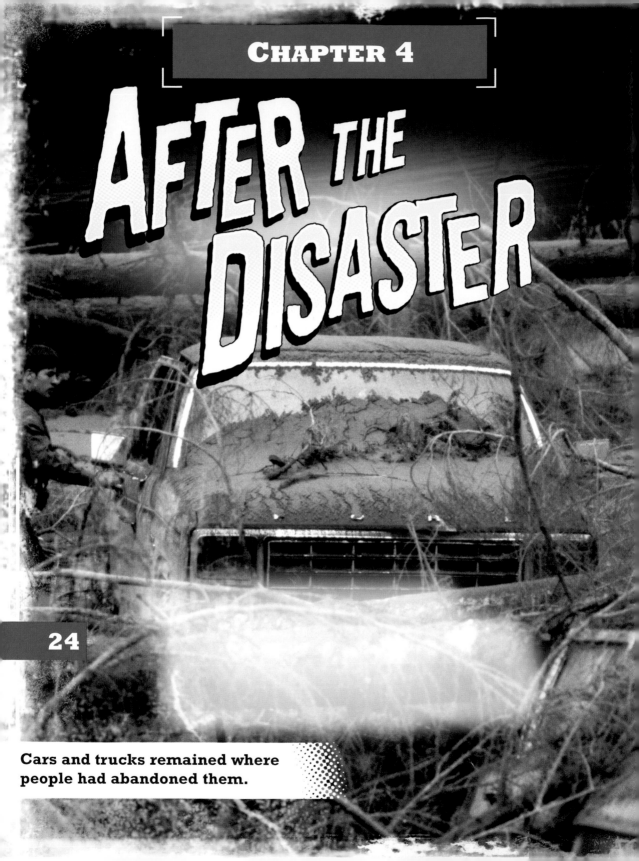

CHAPTER 4

AFTER THE DISASTER

24

Cars and trucks remained where people had abandoned them.

Several months after the disaster, Bruce and Sue returned to the campsite again. The area was spookily quiet. Even the bag of marshmallows still lay where Bruce dropped it.

Bruce and Sue found their truck, which started right away. They then buried Terry and Karen's belongings. As they left the campsite, they tried to pack the disaster away in their memories. But it was hard.

25

Bruce often had dreams about Terry and Karen. Sue dreamed of trying to get people to believe the volcano was about to erupt, but no one would listen.

MOVING INTO THE FUTURE

Bruce and Sue married in 1984. They divorced three years later. Today, Bruce lives in Alaska with his wife, Josephine, and daughter, Marlaina. Sue works in Washington as a massage therapist.

Though they live separate lives, Bruce and Sue are forever linked. They survived one of the most damaging natural disasters in U.S. history. The eruption killed 57 people and destroyed 150 square miles (389 square kilometers) of trees.

Reporters still contact Sue and Bruce to talk about their ordeal. Sue prefers to keep her life private. But Bruce says that talking about the disaster helps him deal with the sadness he still feels.

A year after the eruption, little had changed on the mountain.

27

1983

2004

Today, trees and plants have returned to Mount St. Helens.

In 2000, near the 20th anniversary of the disaster, Bruce took his daughter to the old campsite. Marlaina, who was 11, found a shoe that belonged to one of the campers. Bruce showed Marlaina a zipper from Terry and Karen's tent. Choked up with emotion, Bruce said, "This is tough. This is real tough."

But so were Bruce and Sue. And that toughness helped them survive the disaster and rescue other people. They proved themselves to be heroes as well as survivors.

The mudline on some trees reached at least 60 feet (18 meters).

29

GLOSSARY

cedar (SEE-dur)—a type of evergreen tree with red bark

disaster (duh-ZASS-tur)—an event that causes great damage, loss, or suffering

earthquake (URTH-kwayk)—a sudden, violent shaking of the ground; earthquakes are caused by shifting of the earth's crust.

eruption (i-RUHPT-shuhn)—the action of throwing out rock, hot ash, and lava from a volcano with great force

magma (MAG-muh)—melted rock found under the earth's surface

volcano (vol-KAY-noh)—a mountain with vents through which molten lava, ash, and gas may erupt

READ MORE

Currie, Stephen. *Escapes from Natural Disasters.* Great Escapes. San Diego: Lucent, 2004.

Green, Jen. *Mount St. Helens.* Disasters. Milwaukee: Gareth Stevens, 2005.

Harper, Kristine. *The Mount St. Helens Volcanic Eruption.* Environmental Disasters. New York: Facts on File, 2005.

INTERNET SITES

FactHound offers a safe, fun way to find Internet sites related to this book. All of the sites on FactHound have been researched by our staff.

Here's how:

1. Visit *www.facthound.com*

2. Choose your grade level.

3. Type in this book ID **0736867791** for age-appropriate sites. You may also browse subjects by clicking on letters, or by clicking on pictures and words.

4. Click on the **Fetch It** button.

FactHound will fetch the best sites for you!

31

INDEX